Written by Natoia Franklin   Illu...

Tanika's Unforgettable Dream

This Book belongs to

Name :

....

Address :

....

Copyright© 2021 Serenity Life Fitness Inc.

All rights reserved. No part of this book may be reproduced or used in any manner without the prior written permission of the copyright owner, except for the use of brief quotations in a book review.

To request permissions, contact the publisher at owners@serenitylifefitness.com.

First paperback edition December 2021

Cover art by Endy Astiko
Layout by Endy Astiko

Serenity Life Fitness Inc.
6615 Grand Avenue
#1009
Gurnee, IL 60099

Dedicated to the most beautiful mommy in the world, Beverly Gurley

You are my motivation.

Tanika would never forget the day her best friend went away. It was the saddest day of her life. You see, Tanika's best friend was her mom. Her mom was the best person in the whole wide world. She always had the best jokes and the silliest songs. Whenever Tanika was with her mom, she never wanted to leave her side.

Tanika spent countless days daydreaming about how she and her mom would go shopping together. They would visit Lakehurst Mall, browsing through all the stores, looking for nothing at all. They would go to the movies, slurp on the cherry ICEEs, chomp on cheesy nachos, devour the buttery popcorn, and gobble up all the sweet crunchy butterfingers.

One day, Tanika's mom became sick with a disease. She was so sick that she was continuously rushed to the hospital day after day. This made shopping adventures impossible for Tanika and her mom. Still, her mom continued to fight for her life and would always come home feeling better than when she left. "Mom, you are my hero," Tanika said to her mother one day after she got back from the hospital. But, one terrible day, Tanika's mom didn't come home like she would always do. God took her mom to Heaven instead.

At first, Tanika couldn't believe her mom was gone. "My mom is still coming back...she always does," Tanika said to anyone who cared to listen. She just could not accept that her best friend and hero was gone forever. She couldn't imagine life without her mom. She couldn't even cry, but she was always sad. Even at school, Tanika stopped playing with her friends. She also stopped paying attention in class. Her grades began to drop, so much that her teacher noticed.
"Tanika, are you alright? You have been failing your subjects even when you used to be our brightest student." Her teacher was curious to find out why Tanika, a straight A student, was suddenly failing her classes. "I miss my mom so much," Tanika replied. Her teacher tried to cheer Tanika up.

A couple of weeks passed, and Tanika tried to move on with her life, without her best friend. But her mind was still confused. She and her sisters moved in with their aunt and uncle so that they could be taken care of. The family was very sad. But things were about to change for Tanika. One night Tanika lay on her bed to sleep. When she closed her eyes, her mind began to drift.

"Tanika…Tanika…Tanika," repeated a familiar voice. Tanika opened her eyes to see her mom's round and beautiful face, with her piercing hazel eyes staring back at Tanika. "Mommyyyyyyy," squeaked an enthusiastic Tanika. The two friends embraced. "Tanika, I want you to know you can be anything you want to be. You are my smart and beautiful girl. You have my caring heart, and with that heart, you will change the world. I also want you to know that you are special," Tanika's mom said.
"But mommy, I am so lonely without you by my side," Tanika said, holding on to her mom. "Sometimes you will get lonely because you will feel like no one understands you. You may even feel lost, but through it all, I want you to know I am never really far from you…you have me in your heart…and I will never go away," her mom replied. Suddenly, tears began to trickle from Tanika's cheeks. "But mommy, you left me. That wasn't supposed to happen. We had many places to explore together." "Oh baby," said her mom. "We HAVE many places to explore. You see, whenever you go to the mall, I will be with you to browse through the
stores. When you go to the movies, I will be there chomping the cheesy nachos with you. When you have your first child, I will be there cheering you on. I am ALWAYS THERE with you."

Just then, there was a bright light...so bright that it made Tanika hide her face with her hands. "Tanika, wake up girl. We are going to be late for school," her sister Sharlene said. Tanika realized she had been awakened from a dream. But it wasn't just any dream, it was an unforgettable dream. Tanika smiled and kept that dream to herself, but she was no longer sad and lonely.
One weekend, Tanika remembered the dream. She turned to her sister, with a big smile on her face. "Sharlene! Let's go to the mall," Tanika exclaimed. Tanika was excited to go to the mall again because she knew her mom was always with her. Everyone was surprised at the change, but happy that Tanika was getting back to her old self. At the mall, she ran through the aisles and browsed through the things in the mall, with such excitement.

Everyone was surprised at the change in Tanika, especially at school. "What happened? Your grades are back up! I am happy you are taking your studies seriously," her teacher said with a smile. Tanika smiled and looked up. "See that mommy? I am going to make you proud." Tanika thought this and smiled back at her teacher, as she rubbed her heart. Tanika was inspired to do her best and excelled in all her classes.

One day, Tanika went to the school library and found a little girl crying. "Come on now, why are you here crying?" Tanika asked. "I miss my mommy. She went to heaven and left me all alone," the little girl said. "Don't you know that your mommy is always with you? My mommy went to heaven too, but now she is in my heart. So I am never alone," Tanika said. "Is that so?" The little girl asked. "Yes, it is true. Your mommy is here." Tanika pointed to the girl's heart. The little girl held her heart and smiled. She became happy, knowing that her mother was always with her.

Another day, Tanika went to the restroom during class and found her classmate, Toby, being bullied by the biggest boy in their class. Tanika wanted to help Toby, but was afraid. Then she remembered what her mother said to her. "You can be anything you want to be," her mother had said to her. Tanika decided she would be brave.
"Leave Toby alone and stop bullying him, or I will tell the teacher," Tanika blurted.
The biggest boy ran away because he was afraid. "Thank you, Tanika. You are very brave. I wish I could be brave like you," Toby said. "Remember Toby, you can be anything you want to be." Tanika smiled and walked away.

Tanika went on to become a girl that her family was proud of. She graduated high school with honors and went to college. In college, she was also a straight A student and earned several degrees. In all, her mother was her motivation. Whenever she visited a new place she was sure to rub her heart…the place where her best friend lived. She realized she was never alone and spent the rest of her days exploring the world with her best friend. Knowing that her mom was always with her gave Tanika strength to conquer the world.

Author Page

Natoia Franklin is an educator, Holistic Health Coach, personal trainer, and group fitness extraordinaire for women and children. As the owner of Serenity Life Fitness and co-founder of RHYTHM Academy, she offers services that inspire physical, mental, and spiritual transformation. She is passionate about serving underserved communities while ensuring that those communities get access and exposure to effective wellness programs that target obesity, poor nutrition, mental health issues, and sedentary lifestyles. When she is not training or teaching, she is busy being a mom to her four children and wife to her husband. Website: www.serenitylifefitness.com

Made in the USA
Middletown, DE
11 May 2022